From the Library of:

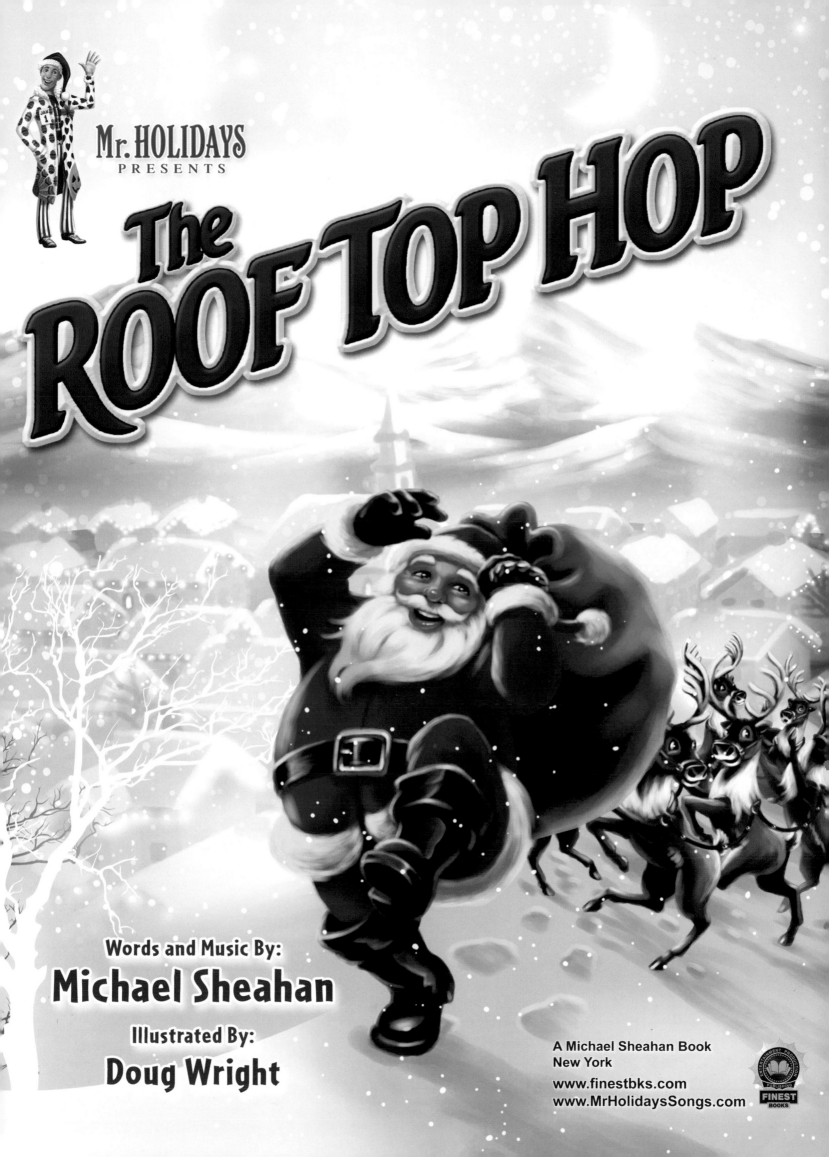

Mr. HOLIDAYS
PRESENTS

The ROOF TOP HOP

Words and Music By:
Michael Sheahan

Illustrated By:
Doug Wright

A Michael Sheahan Book
New York

www.finestbks.com
www.MrHolidaysSongs.com

FINEST
BOOKS

Hello boys and girls …
My name is Mr. Holidays.

Do I have a secret to share with you!
Did you know that Santa
has a favorite song?

Did you know that Santa
dances to that song on your
roof top every Christmas Eve?

Well, let it be a secret no more,
as I invite you to read, sing and dance
along to Santa's favorite song!

Now, I know you heard
the sleigh bells
when Santa comes along.

Well, now it's time to let
you in on Santa's favorite song.

Oh, I bet you didn't know ...
How Santa likes to go.

Delivering his toys ...
To all the little girls and boys.

It's a rhythm in his feet.
Yes, he moves to his own beat
as he glides across ice and snow
all the elves and reindeer know.

How Santa does The Roof Top Hop
from house to house he doesn't stop.

With sleigh bells jingling to the beat
of the reindeer's pitter-patter
and from Santa's feet.

Down the chimney Santa goes
with fire beneath his toes.

Yeah, he's real quick on his feet,
and don't forget to leave that treat.

'Cause he needs his energy
to climb up that chimney.

And, cool his feet off in the snow
to the dance that you now know.

When Santa does The Roof Top Hop
from house to house he doesn't stop.
With sleigh bells jingling to the beat
of the reindeer's pitter-patter,
and from Santa's feet.

16

It's like he's dancing …
dancing on a cloud.

'Cause it never gets too loud.

It's a hip hop … bebop … rock 'n' roll,
that brings joy and happiness
to every soul.

When Santa does The Roof Top Hop
from house to house he doesn't stop.
With sleigh bells jingling to the beat
of the reindeer's pitter-patter,
and from Santa's feet.

Now, next time you hear sleigh bells,
when Santa comes along,
shake your hips and move your feet
to Santa's favorite song.

When Santa does The Roof Top Hop
from house to house he doesn't stop.
With sleigh bells jingling to the beat
of the reindeer's pitter-patter,
and from Santa's feet.

When Santa does The Roof Top Hop
from house to house he doesn't stop.

When Santa does The Roof Top Hop
from house to house he doesn't stop.

When Santa does The Roof Top Hop
from house to house he doesn't stop.

When Santa does The Roof Top Hop
from house to house he doesn't stop.

When Santa does The Roof Top Hop
from house to house he doesn't stop.

When Santa does The Roof Top Hop
from house to house he doesn't stop.

For my wife Barbara who inspired the dance.

For my sons Michael, Joseph and Gabriel…who keep me young!

To Mom and Dad, and fathers and mothers everywhere,
for making fond memories, and keeping the holidays special.

Library of Congress Control Number: 2010930756

Published by Finest Books Inc., 959 West Jericho Turnpike, Smithtown, NY 11787

Words & Music by Michael Sheahan

Copyright © 2009 Finest Music, Inc. d/b/a Do Well Publishing (BMI)

All rights reserved. Used by permission.

Illustrations by Doug Wright © 2010 by Finest Books, Inc.

Designed by Sharon Baldino

Distributed in the United States by AtlasBooks Distribution Services, Inc.

30 Amberwood Parkway, Ashland, OH 44805

Distributed in Canada by AtlasBooks Distribution Services, Inc.

Printed in China

July 2010 Batch #A29

Finest ISBN 13: 978-1-935679-00-4

For information about custom editions, special sales, premium and corporate purchases,
please contact Finest Books, Inc. at **specialsales@finestbks.com** or **www.finestbks.com**.

For all products presented by Mr. Holidays go to **www.MrHolidaysSongs.com**.